This Little Tiger
book belongs to:

_____

_____

_____

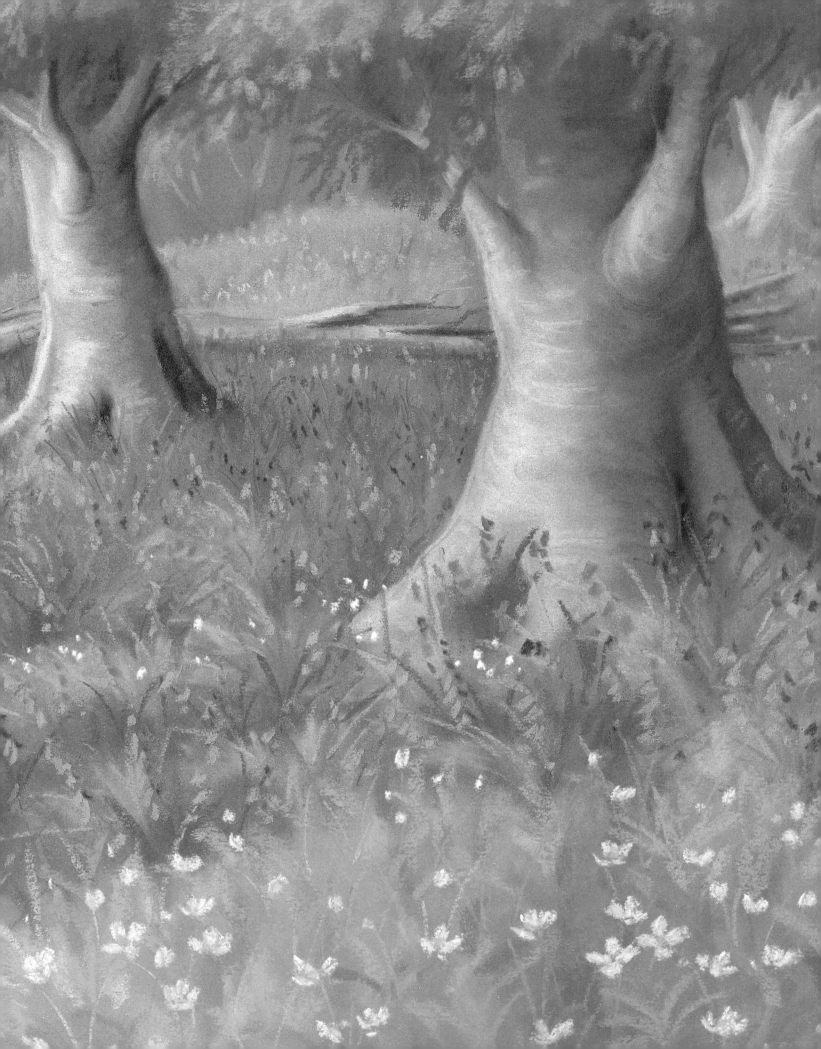

For Finn and George, with love ~ M C B

To my Grandfather Hakon Kristensen ~ T M

LITTLE TIGER PRESS
An imprint of Magi Publications
1 The Coda Centre, 189 Munster Road, London SW6 6AW
www.littletigerpress.com

First published in Great Britain 2010
This edition published 2010

Text copyright © M Christina Butler 2010
Illustrations copyright © Tina Macnaughton 2010
M Christina Butler and Tina Macnaughton have asserted their
rights to be identified as the author and illustrator of this work
under the Copyright, Designs and Patents Act, 1988

A CIP catalogue record for this book is available from the
British Library

Printed in China

10 9 8 7 6 5 4 3 2 1

One Special Day

M Christina Butler

Illustrated by Tina Macnaughton

LITTLE TIGER PRESS
London

Spring was here at last and Little
Hedgehog was very excited.
  *"The sun is shining, off we go –
    To find out where the bluebells grow!"*
he sang, merrily packing his lunch.
    Just then, he heard a voice
calling outside.

It was Ma and Baby Hedgehog.

"Could you look after Baby?" asked Ma anxiously. "I must take care of Mole. He has a dreadful cold."

"Dear, dear!" replied Little Hedgehog. "Of course!"

"Thank you," she said, giving Baby a big kiss. And off she went.

"We're hunting for bluebells today, Baby!"
smiled Little Hedgehog.
    "Whee!" squeaked Baby Hedgehog, as they
set off together. "Baby's hunting bluebells!
And Blankie's coming too!"

Badger, Fox and Mouse soon joined them.

"This is my baby cousin," said Little Hedgehog. "He's coming along to help."

"Very nice," nodded Badger, taking the lead.

"A baby?" frowned Fox. "And what's that *thing* he's holding?"

"It's my blankie!" giggled Baby Hedgehog.

"We'll find the best bluebells in Wild Flower Woods," began Little Hedgehog.

"I see one!" squeaked Baby Hedgehog, running off into a bramble patch.

"Baby! Come back!" cried Little Hedgehog.

"Don't worry, he won't be far away," said Badger, as they all began searching through the brambles.

All at once Baby Hedgehog pattered out
covered in leaves. "For you!" he beamed,
holding out a big, blue feather.
   "Thank you, that's lovely, Baby . . .
but where's your blankie?" said
Little Hedgehog.

"My blankie!" cried Baby
Hedgehog in a panic. "I've
lost my blankie!"

"Oh no!" groaned Fox.

"It's all right, Baby," said Little
Hedgehog gently. "We'll find Blankie."
And they began searching the
brambles again.

"I've found it!" Mouse's voice
came at last. But as she tugged at
the blanket, suddenly the bramble
sprung back . . . PING!

BUMP!

Mouse fell on her bottom,
and the blanket went sailing
up in the air!

"Blankie, come back!"
squeaked Baby Hedgehog.

Just as the blanket floated to the ground, Baby Hedgehog dived onto it, and went bumping and bouncing in a blankety ball down the hillside.

"He'll hurt himself! Stop him!" cried Little Hedgehog, running after Baby.

"Here we go again," puffed Fox, joining in the chase.

The blankety ball rolled to a stop and
Baby tumbled out among the primroses.

"Oh Baby!" gasped Little Hedgehog.
"Thank goodness you're safe!"
"Baby likes hunting bluebells!"
laughed Baby, as they hugged each other.

"Would you believe it?" smiled Little Hedgehog. "We've reached Wild Flower Woods!"

"Ready, steady, go!" Badger cried, and off they ran to see who would find the bluebells first.

"Over there!" Mouse shouted out.
"I've found them . . .

EEEEEK!"

"Whatever was that?" exclaimed Fox.
"It was Mouse!" cried Little Hedgehog.
"Come on, we must help!"

Mouse had fallen into a deep, dark hole.
  "It must be an old rabbit warren,"
muttered Badger.
  "Hold on!" called Little Hedgehog.
"We'll soon get you out."

Little Hedgehog, Badger and Fox tried and tried but the hole was just too deep to reach Mouse.

Then Baby Hedgehog got very excited. "Blankie will get Mousie out," he cried.

"That's it!" said Badger. "We'll pull her out with the blanket!"

"Well done, Baby!" said Little Hedgehog proudly.

Little Hedgehog and Baby held on to
the blanket tightly and Mouse caught
hold of it.

"One! Two! Three! *Pull*!" cried
Little Hedgehog. Then everyone
tugged, and with one
mighty heave . . .

Mouse popped up out of the hole!
"Hurrah!" they shouted, giggling
and falling back together.

"We found the bluebells," chuckled Badger,
"but what a day!"

"And what a hero!" Fox smiled at Baby.
"Just like your big cousin, Little Hedgehog!"

And chattering and laughing, they all sat
down together for a special picnic amongst
the bluebells.

Look out for more SPECIAL reads
from Little Tiger Press

Rhino's Great BIG Itch!
Natalie Chivers

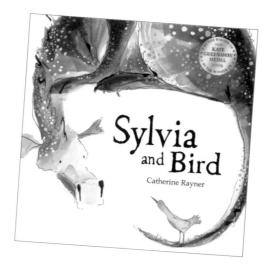

Sylvia and Bird
Catherine Rayner

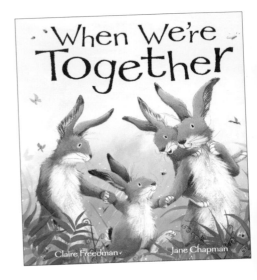

When We're Together
Claire Freedman · Jane Chapman

Time for Bed, Little One
Caroline Pitcher · Tina Macnaughton

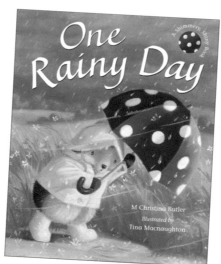

One Rainy Day
A Shimmery, Shiny Book
M Christina Butler
Illustrated by Tina Macnaughton

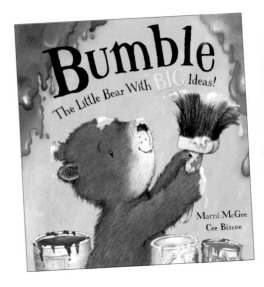

Bumble
The Little Bear With BIG Ideas!
Marni McGee · Cee Biscoe

For information regarding any of the above titles
or for our catalogue, please contact us:
Little Tiger Press, 1 The Coda Centre,
189 Munster Road, London SW6 6AW
Tel: 020 7385 6333
Fax: 020 7385 7333
E-mail: info@littletiger.co.uk
www.littletigerpress.com